This book belongs to:

....

....

For my Ann

Quarto is the authority on a wide range of topics.

Quarto educates, entertains and enriches the lives of our readers—enthusiasts and lovers of hands-on living. www.quartoknows.com

Author and Illustrator: Steve Smallman
Designer: Victoria Kimonidou
Editor: Harriet Stone

This edition first published in 2019 by QEB Publishing,
an imprint of The Quarto Group.
26391 Crown Valley Parkway, Suite 220
Mission Viejo, CA 92691, USA
T: +1 949 380 7510
F: +1 949 380 7575
www.QuartoKnows.com

A CIP record for this book is available from the Library of Congress.

ISBN 978 0 7112 4335 4

Manufactured in Shenzhen, China PP092019

9 8 7 6 5 4 3 2 1

Kind Mr. Bear

BY STEVE SMALLMAN

Mr. Bear was very kind.

When anyone met him walking in the woods,
he would raise his hat, say *"Good morning!"*
and smile his warm crinkly smile.
He was always happy to help.

Mr. Bear helped the animals reach things that were high up.

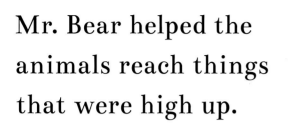

He carried things they couldn't lift.

He sheltered them from the rain.

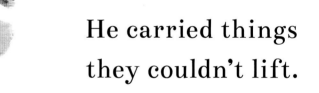

And he tidied up after parties when everyone else was heading home. He never made a fuss about helping anyone. He just got on with it.

But because Mr. Bear had been in the forest for as long as anyone could remember, the animals started to take his help for granted. Nobody even remembered to say *thank you* anymore.

Mr. Bear got very tired and a little bit sad.

And then he got sick.

His nose was runny, his head ached, and he was very cold. His fire had gone out, but he felt too ill to fetch firewood.

Mr. Bear lay on his bed
in his cave, all alone.

And for a long time
nobody seemed to care.

A tree had fallen onto Mr. Badger's garden.

"*Can you move this tree,
Mr. Bear?*" he asked.

But Mr. Bear wasn't there.

Squirrel had collected a big sack
full of nuts, but it was too heavy
to lift up to his treetop house.

"Lift these nuts up, Mr. Bear!"
called Squirrel.

But Mr. Bear wasn't there.

A family of mice were caught out in the rain.

"*Mr. Bear! Mr. Bear!*
We're getting wet!" they cried.

But Mr. Bear wasn't there.

"Humph!" grumbled Mrs. Mouse.
*"I'm soaked! Where's that bear
when we need him?"*

They squelched home feeling very grumpy.

But the smallest mouse was worried. She hurried off to Mr. Bear's cave and found him looking pale and ill and shivering with cold.

"*Oh dear!*" she gasped.
"*Are you all right?*"

"*Not really, my dear,
but thank you for asking,*"
whispered Mr. Bear.

The little mouse ran through
the forest knocking on all the doors.

"What do you want?"
cried the animals.

"It's Mr. Bear. He's sick!"

"Sick?" Squirrel cried. "But he's never sick!
He's always there to help us."

"Yes, but who is there to help him?"
asked the little mouse.

The animals felt ashamed. They remembered
all the things that Mr. Bear had done for them,
and how little they had done in return.

Later that day, Mr. Bear was surprised
to see all his neighbors at his door.

Mr. Badger had
brought some wood
and soon had a fire
going in the hearth.

Squirrel had brought a bowl of his best nuts
and Mrs. Rabbit had made a big pot of carrot soup.

The mice carried in a large
blanket and soon Mr. Bear
was snuggled up feeling
as warm as toast.

The animals took turns sitting with Mr. Bear and they looked after him until he was better.

Mr. Bear still helps the other animals whenever he can, but now...the animals help him back!

Because that's what friends do.

NEXT STEPS

Discussion and Comprehension

Discuss the story with the children and ask the following questions, encouraging them to take turns and give answers in full sentences if they are able to. Offer support by turning to the appropriate pages of the book if needed.

- What did you like most about this story?
- In what ways was Mr. Bear kind?
- What do you understand by taking someone for granted? Do you think you have ever done this?
- Why did the animals feel ashamed?
- What makes a good friend?
- Do you think that everyone was happy at the end of the story? Why?

Character Descriptions

Give each child a piece of paper divided into four boxes with a circle in the middle. Label the four boxes in advance for the children: What does he look like? Who are his friends? What problems does he face? What do you know about him? Ask the children to draw a picture of Kind Mr. Bear in the circle in the center of the paper and write his name underneath. Reinforce some of the phrases that the author used to describe Mr. Bear's appearance and character: "warm crinkly smile," "never made a fuss." Encourage and support the children to write a sentence under the heading in each box, using copies of the book to help them. When the children have finished, encourage them to read out their character descriptions of Mr. Bear.

Fork Paintings

Show the children pictures of Mr. Bear in the book. Show how his fur isn't smooth, especially at the edges. Give the children a large piece of light brown sugar paper and a template of Mr. Bear to draw around. Give them pots of brown paint, paint brushes, and plastic forks. Encourage them to paint Mr. Bear and use the forks to paint around the edge to create the appearance and texture of fur. Once the paintings are dry, allow the children to draw on eyes, nose, mouth, and eyeglasses with black and gray felt pens. Display alongside the character descriptions above.